BARTHOLOMEW and the OOBLECK

Written and illustrated

BY Dr. SEUSS

RANDOM HOUSE NEW YORK

For

KELVIN C. VANDERLIP, JR.

This title was originally cataloged by the Library of Congress as follows:
[Geisel, Theodor Seuss] 1904–   Bartholomew and the oobleck; written and illustrated by
Dr. Seuss [pseud.] New York, Random House [1949]   [48] p. illus. (part col.) 31 cm.
I. Title.   PZ8.G326Bar   49-11423   ISBN: 0-394-80075-3   0-394-90075-8 (lib. bdg.)

Manufactured in the United States of America

THEY still talk about it in the Kingdom of Didd as The-Year-the-King-Got-Angry-with-the-Sky. And they still talk about the page boy, Bartholomew Cubbins. If it hadn't been for Bartholomew Cubbins, that King and that Sky would have wrecked that little Kingdom.

Bartholomew had seen the King get angry many, many times before. But *that* year when His Majesty started growling at the *sky,* Bartholomew Cubbins just didn't know what to make of it.

Yet all that year, the old King did it. All year long he stared up into the air above his kingdom, muttering and sputtering through his royal whiskers, "Humph! The things that come down from my sky!"

All spring when the rain came down, he growled at *that . . .*

All summer when the sunshine came down, he growled at *that* . . .

All autumn when the fog came down,
he growled at *that* . . .

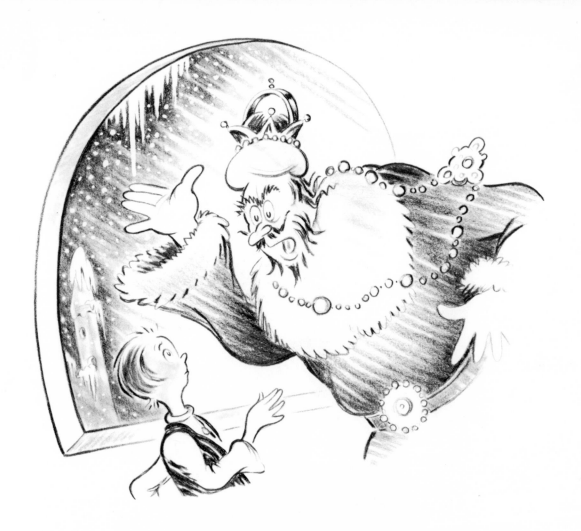

And that winter when the snow came down, he started shouting! "This snow! This fog! This sunshine! This rain! BAHH! These four things that come down from my sky!"

"But, King Derwin," Bartholomew tried to calm him. "You've *always* had these same four things come down."

"That's just the trouble!" bellowed the King. "Every year the *same* four things! I'm mighty tired of those old things! I want something NEW to come down!"

"Something *new* come down . . . ?" Bartholomew gasped. "That's impossible, Your Majesty. You just can't have it."

"Boy, don't you dare tell me what I can or cannot have! Remember, Bartholomew, I am King!"

"I know, Sire," said Bartholomew. "You rule all the land. And you rule all the people. But even kings can't rule the *sky.*"

"Can't, eh?" His Majesty flew into a terrible rage. "Well, maybe *other* kings can't do it, but maybe I'm one king who can! You mark my words, Bartholomew Cubbins, I *will* have something new come down!"

But *how* to get something new to come down . . . ? That was rather hard to think up. And for many days the old King stomped around, trying to figure out *some* way to do it.

Then, finally, late one night, when all the lords and ladies of the palace were fast asleep . . . just as the King was buttoning his royal nightshirt . . . he suddenly stopped still. A strange wild light began to shine in his gray-green eyes.

"Why, of course!" He began laughing. *"They* can do it for me! Bartholomew Cubbins, blow my secret whistle! Quick! Call my royal magicians!"

"Your *magicians,* Your Majesty?" Bartholomew shivered. "Oh, no, Your Majesty! Don't call *them!"*

"You hold your tongue, Bartholomew Cubbins! You do as I command you. Blow my secret whistle!"

"Yes, Sire," Bartholomew bowed. "But, Your Majesty, I still think that you may be very sorry."

He took the King's secret whistle from its secret hook. He blew a long, low blast down the King's back secret stairway.

And a moment later he heard them coming! Up from their musty hole beneath the dungeon, up the empty midnight tunnel to the royal bedchamber tower, came the magicians on their padded, shuffling feet. Up and right into the room they came chanting:

"Shuffle, duffle, muzzle, muff.
Fista, wista, mista-cuff.
We are men of groans and howls,
Mystic men who eat boiled owls.
Tell us what you wish, oh King.
Our magic can do anything."

"I wish," spoke the King, "to have you make something fall from my skies that no other kingdom has ever had before. What can you do? What will you make?"

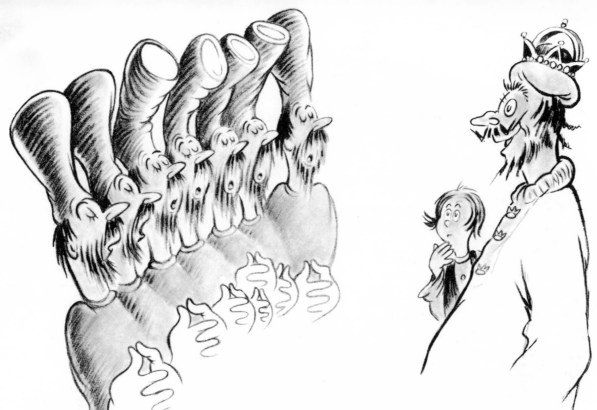

For a moment they stood thinking, blinking their creaky
eyes. Then they spoke a word . . . one word . . . "Oobleck."

"Oobleck . . . ?" asked the King. "What will it look like?"

> "Won't look like rain. Won't look like snow.
> Won't look like fog. That's all we know.
> We just can't tell you any more.
> We've never made oobleck before."

They bowed. They started toward the door.

> "We go now to our secret cave
> On Mystic Mountain Neeka-tave.
> There, all night long, we'll work for you
> And you'll have oobleck when we're through!"

"They'll do something crazy!" whispered Bartholomew.
"Call them back, Your Majesty! Stop them!"

"Stop them? Not for a ton of diamonds!" chuckled the
King. "Why, I'll be the mightiest man that ever lived! Just
think of it! Tomorrow I'm going to have OOBLECK!"

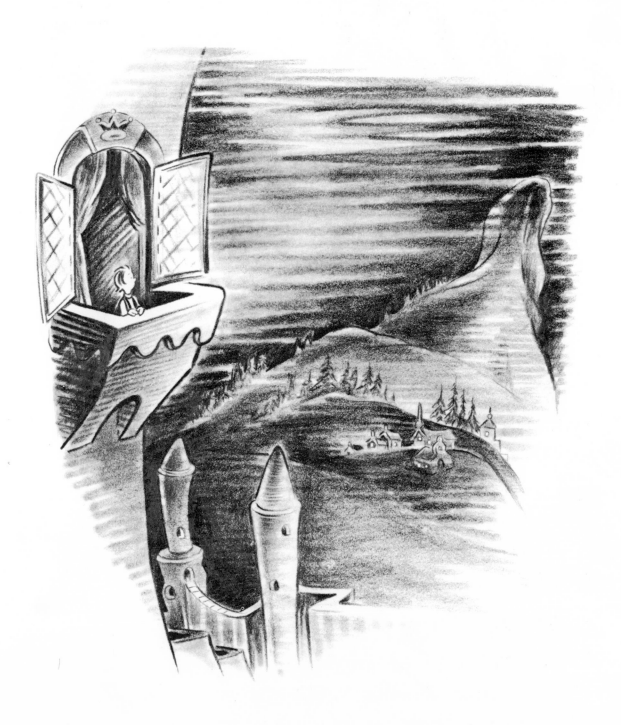

It took Bartholomew a long time to get the excited King to sleep that night. But there was no sleep for Bartholomew, the page boy. All night long he stood in the King's window, staring out at the Mystic Mountain Neeka-tave. Somewhere up there, Bartholomew knew, the magicians were working their terrible magic.

All night the magicians did. All night they walked circles round their magic fire, making magic mumbling with their clucking tongues:

"Oh, snow and rain are not enough!
Oh, we must make some brand-new stuff!
So feed the fire with wet mouse hair,
Burn an onion. Burn a chair.
Burn a whisker from your chin
And burn a long sour lizard skin.
Burn yellow twigs and burn red rust
And burn a stocking full of dust.
Make magic smoke, green, thick and hot!
(It sure smells dreadful, does it not?)
That means the smoke is now just right
So, quick! Before the day gets light,
Go, magic smoke! Go high! Go high!
Go rise into the kingdom's sky!
Go make the oobleck tumble down
On every street, in every town!
Go make the wondrous oobleck fall!
Oh, bring down oobleck on us all!"

Dawn was just breaking and Bartholomew was still standing . . . trembling, watching at the bedchamber window. But now, as the sun rose, Bartholomew smiled. Those silly magicians hadn't done a thing!

Then, suddenly, Bartholomew Cubbins stopped smiling.

Was he seeing things . . . ? No! There *was* something strange up there in the sky!

At first it seemed like a little greenish cloud . . . just a wisp of greenish steam. But now it was coming lower, closer, down toward the fields and farms and houses of the sleeping little kingdom.

It was swirling around the topmost turrets of the palace. Tiny little greenish specks were shimmering in the air right

over his head. Queer little greenish blobs, just about the size of grape seeds!

He stretched out his hand. He started to catch one. Then he pulled his hand back! There was something frightening about those blobs. Bartholomew slammed the window shut.

"Wake up, Your Majesty!" he shouted. "Your oobleck! It's falling!"

The King sprang out of his royal bed sheets.

"By my royal whiskers, it is!" he cried. "Oh, that beautiful oobleck! And it's mine! All mine!"

"I don't like the looks of those blobs, Sire," said Bartholomew. "They're coming down now as big as greenish peanuts."

"The bigger the better!" laughed the King. "Oh, what a day! I'm going to make it a holiday! I want every man, woman and child in my kingdom to go out and dance in my glorious oobleck!"

"Out in *that* stuff . . . ?" asked Bartholomew. "Do you really think it's safe, Sire?"

"Stop asking foolish questions!" snapped the King. "Boy, you run to my royal bell tower. Wake my royal bell ringer. Tell him to ring the great holiday bell!"

For a moment Bartholomew Cubbins didn't move.

"Run!" barked the King. Bartholomew ran.

Across the sleeping palace, Bartholomew ran. Then up the ladder of the high bell tower, he climbed to the bell ringer's little cubbyhole in the belfry.

"Ring your bell!" he called. "His Majesty the King proclaims today a holiday!"

The old man crawled out of his cot. He grabbed the bell
rope. "What's the holiday for, Bartholomew?"

"You'll find out soon enough!" said Bartholomew.

The bell ringer yanked the rope. Nothing happened.

He yanked it harder. Still nothing happened.

"Heh . . . ? What's wrong with my bell?" he murmured.
"I'd better take a look outside."

He poked his head out through the little trap door.

"Merciful gracious!" he gulped. "What is THAT? All over my bell like greenish molasses!"

"Not only your bell!" Bartholomew cried. "Look at that poor robin down there in that tree! She's stuck to her nest! She can't move a wing! That oobleck's gooey! It's gummy! It's like glue!"

"Oooh!" The bell ringer wrung his hands. "If that green stuff sticks up *robins*, it'll stick up *people*, too!"

"Someone's got to warn the people!" cried Bartholomew. "Got to wake 'em and warn 'em to stay inside their houses! I'll tell the royal trumpeter!" he shouted. He turned and slid like lightning down the bell tower ladder.

To the trumpeter's tower raced
Bartholomew Cubbins, and on up
the steps four stairs at a time.

As he ran he could hear the
"*Plop! Plop!*" of the oobleck on
the windowpanes. It was pelting
against the palace walls as big as
greenish cup-cakes now!

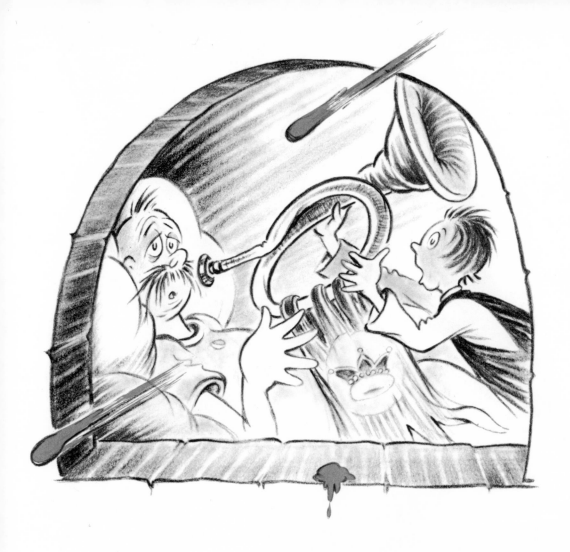

He yanked the covers off the snoring trumpeter. He shoved
his cold trumpet right into his sleepy hands.

"Get up! Warn the people! Blow the alarm!"

"Alarm . . . ?" yawned the trumpeter. Then his eyes saw
the oobleck. "Those green things, Bartholomew! Where'd
they come from?"

"The King . . ." panted Bartholomew. "His royal magicians made them!"

The royal trumpeter leapt from his bed. "That King of
ours should be ashamed!" He jabbed his trumpet out of the
window. "I'll blow," he shouted, "the loudest alarm that's
ever been heard in the Kingdom of Didd!"

But all the royal trumpeter blew was a "GLUGG!"

"My horn!" he gulped. "One of those green things flew in-side it!"

He tried to blow it out. He couldn't blow it out.

He tried to shake it out. He couldn't shake it out.

"I'll get it *somehow!*" he yelled. "I'll *pull* it out!"

"No!" shouted Bartholomew. "Don't you touch it!"

The trumpeter's hand was already in it. His fingers grabbed hold of the lump of oobleck. He could feel it squiggle around in his fist like a slippery potato dumpling made of rubber.

He pulled with all his might. The oobleck began to stretch. Then, *"Gloing!"* the oobleck snapped back inside the trumpet. It yanked his arm back with it right up to the elbow.

"I can't wiggle a finger!" the trumpeter wailed. "Oh, Bartholomew, what'll I do?"

"I don't know. And I hate to leave you stuck to your horn. But if *you* can't warn the people of the kingdom, I've got to find someone who can!"

Out of the room and down the stairs raced Bartholomew Cubbins . . .

. . . down to the chamber of the Captain of the Guards. The Captain was humming in front of his mirror, combing the ends of his handsome moustache.

"Captain! DO something!" shouted Bartholomew.

"Do something? Why?" smiled the Captain. "What's wrong?"

"Captain! Haven't you seen the dreadful oobleck? It's coming down now as big as greenish baseballs!"

"Oh, *that* stuff," laughed the Captain. "What's so dreadful about that, lad? You know, *I* think it's rather pretty."

"Captain!" pleaded Bartholomew. "It's dangerous!"

"Nonsense!" snorted the Captain. "Lad, are you trying to frighten *me*? Captains, my boy, are afraid of nothing. That stuff's harmless. I'll show you. I'll eat some."

"*Eat* some . . . ?" gasped Bartholomew. "Oh, *no!*"

But before Bartholomew could stop him, the Captain was leaning out his window, scooping up some oobleck on the end of his sword.

"Don't, Captain! DON'T!"

The Captain did! By the time Bartholomew dragged him back inside the room, his mouth was glued tight shut with oobleck. He tried to speak, but no words came out. All the noble Captain of the Guards could do was blow a lot of little sticky greenish bubbles.

"Forgive me for leaving you, Captain," said Bartholomew. "But a captain full of bubbles is no help at all." Bartholomew stretched the poor man out. He left him there on his chamber floor.

Bartholomew went tearing through the zigzag palace hallways. "I'll get the King's horse! I'll ride through the country! I'll warn the people of the kingdom myself!"

He pushed open the door that led out to the Royal Stables.

Bartholomew stopped. He could go no farther. The awful oobleck was plumping down as big as greenish footballs now!

Too late to warn the people of the kingdom! There were farmers in the fields, getting stuck to hoes and plows. Goats were getting stuck to ducks. Geese were getting stuck to cows.

Outside the palace it was piling up, great greenish tons of oobleck, deeper and deeper on every roof in the land.

There was nothing Bartholomew Cubbins could do out there. Shaking his head sadly, he stepped back inside.

But inside, a moment later, it was just as bad as out!

With an angry roar, the oobleck was suddenly hitting the palace harder. It was battering and spattering against the walls as big as greenish buckets full of gooey asparagus soup!

Like a sinking sailboat, the whole palace was springing leaks. The oobleck was ripping the windows right off their hinges.

It was dripping through the ceilings. It was rolling down the chimneys. It was coming in everywhere . . . even through the keyholes!

From every bedroom in the palace came the howls of lords and ladies. Frightened, in their nightgowns, they came jumping to their doors.

"Go back to your beds! Get under your blankets!" Bartholomew Cubbins went crying through the halls.

But nobody paid the slightest attention. Everyone in the palace started rushing madly about.

The Royal Cook rushed down to the royal kitchen. Bartholomew Cubbins saw him trapped there, stuck to three stew pots, a tea cup and a cat!

The Royal Laundress rushed outside to save her laundry. Bartholomew saw her, stuck tight to the clothesline, between two woolen stockings and the King's best Sunday blouse!

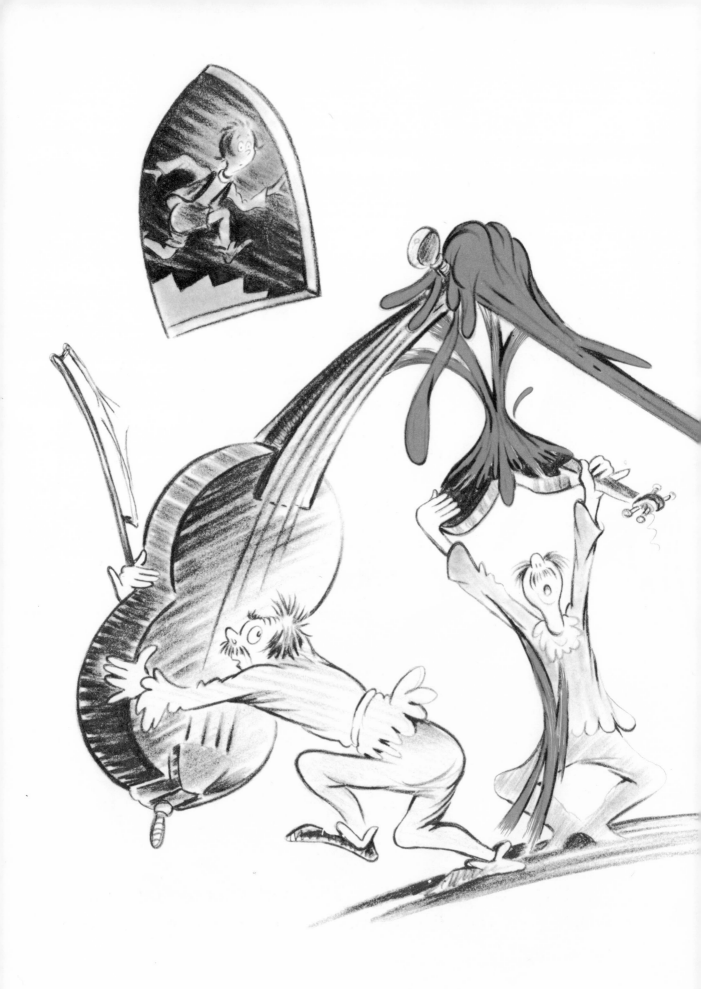

He saw the Royal Fiddlers. They were stuck to their royal fiddles! Everywhere Bartholomew ran, he saw someone stuck to something!

They were stuck up by the dozens! Every last friend he had
in the world was flopping and floundering, all hopelessly
caught in the goo.

Then, suddenly midst the hubbub, Bartholomew gasped,
"*The King!*" Where *was* the King? He'd forgotten all about
him!

It was in the throne room that Bartholomew found him.

There he sat . . . Old King Derwin, proud and mighty ruler of the Kingdom of Didd, trembling, shaking, helpless as a baby.

His royal crown was stuck to his royal head. The seat of his royal pants were stuck to his royal throne. Oobleck was dripping from his royal eyebrows. It was oozing into his royal ears.

"Fetch my magicians, Bartholomew!" he commanded. "Make them say some magic words! Make them stop the oobleck falling!"

Bartholomew shrugged his shoulders. "I can't fetch them, Your Majesty. Their cave on Mountain Neeka-tave is buried deep in oobleck."

"Then *I* must think of some magic words!" groaned the King. "Oh, what are those words my magicians say . . . ? *Shuffle . . . duffle . . . muzzle . . . muff* . . . That's all I can remember and they don't do any good! The oobleck keeps on falling harder!"

Bartholomew Cubbins could hold his tongue no longer.

"And it's going to keep on falling," he shouted, "until your whole great marble palace tumbles down! So don't waste your time saying foolish *magic* words. YOU ought to be saying some plain *simple* words!"

"*Simple* words . . . ? What do you mean, boy?"

"I mean," said Bartholomew, "this is all *your* fault! Now, the least you can do is say the simple words, 'I'm sorry'."

No one had ever talked to the King like this before.

"What!" he bellowed. "ME . . . *ME* say I'm sorry! Kings *never* say 'I'm sorry!' And I am the mightiest king in all the world!"

Bartholomew looked the King square in the eye.

"You may be a mighty king," he said. "But you're sitting in oobleck up to your chin. And so is everyone else in your land. And if you won't even say you're sorry, *you're no sort of a king at all!*"

Bartholomew Cubbins turned his back. He started for the throne room door.

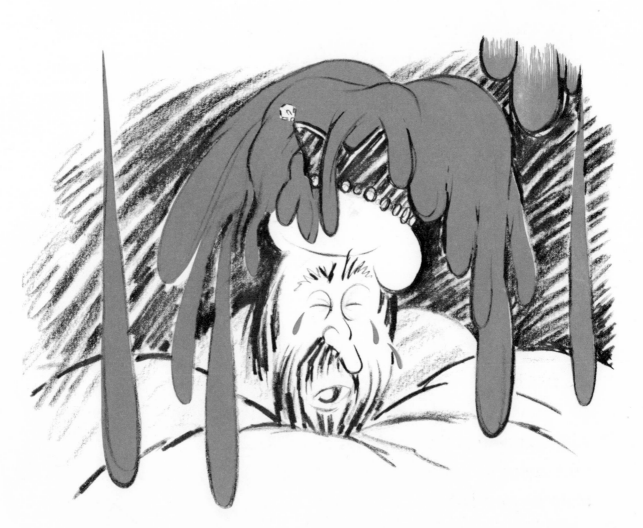

But then Bartholomew heard a great, deep sob. The old King was crying! "Come back, Bartholomew Cubbins! You're right! It *is* all my fault! And I *am* sorry! Oh, Bartholomew, I'm awfully, *awfully* sorry!"

And the moment the King spoke those words, something happened . . .

Maybe there *was* something magic in those simple words, "I'm sorry."

Maybe there *was* something magic in those simple words, "It's all my fault."

Maybe there was, and maybe there wasn't. But they say that as soon as the old King spoke them, the sun began to shine and fight its way through the storm. They say that the falling oobleck blobs grew smaller and smaller and smaller.

They say that all the oobleck that was stuck on all the people and on all the animals of the Kingdom of Didd just simply, quietly melted away.

And then, they say, Bartholomew took the old King by the sleeve . . .

... and led him up the steps of the high bell tower. He put the bell rope into His Majesty's royal hands and the King himself rang the holiday bell.

Then the King proclaimed a brand-new national holiday ... in honor of the four perfect things that come down from the sky.

The King now knew that these four old-fashioned things ... the rain, the sunshine, the fog and the snow ... were good enough for any king in all the world, especially for him, old King Derwin of Didd.